RISHABH PANT

INDIAN CRICKETER

MR VIVEK KUMAR PANDEY

AF375293

Copyright © Mr Vivek Kumar Pandey
All Rights Reserved.

This book has been published with all efforts taken to make the material error-free after the consent of the author. However, the author and the publisher do not assume and hereby disclaim any liability to any party for any loss, damage, or disruption caused by errors or omissions, whether such errors or omissions result from negligence, accident, or any other cause.

While every effort has been made to avoid any mistake or omission, this publication is being sold on the condition and understanding that neither the author nor the publishers or printers would be liable in any manner to any person by reason of any mistake or omission in this publication or for any action taken or omitted to be taken or advice rendered or accepted on the basis of this work. For any defect in printing or binding the publishers will be liable only to replace the defective copy by another copy of this work then available.

During Writing This Book No character & No religious ,
No Relation Members Are Harmed. It's Only For Study
Purpose.Only Short Biography Of Rishabh Pant & Life
Style,Carreer etc.

Contents

Foreword

Author biography in English :

MY NAME IS VIVEK KUMAR PANDEY . I WAS BORN IN 30 SEP 2002,I AM FROM SURAT GUJARAT INDIA.MY DREAM WAS TO BE GOOD WRITERS ,MY FAMILY SUPPORTED ME TO SUCCESSFUL AND I CAN DO IT MY SELF.How do I write? That is a question, I believe, that can be honestly answered by me."CELEBRATING YOUNGEST WRITER AWARD WINNER IN GUJARAT 1ST RANK" MR PANDEY JI . I may think I did a good job writing something. The reader is the one who decides the quality of my writing. I do find writing to be natural to me and therefore find it to be a real challenge. My trick as a challenged writer is to do the best I can and know that I am happy with the final outcome. It may take a while to do my best and there may be quite a few problems I run into along the way.

I am not a greedy person those who are thinking about me and my self I never tried it anyone people suffering from sadness ,I trying to get promoted people suffering from happiness and joy in your Life Time. Now in current situation in India and also world people are unemployed and have no many but our indian governor help to people to get free food from ration card , i also take part in leadership team ,i am Motivational speaker , Film script writer. There was my two dream firstly writer and secondly actor & also my own film is upcoming soon i done almost completely completed script for my film .I AM GOING TO SAY WORD OF HEART TOUCH OUT PLEASE READ IT" , firstly i thanks my father he supports me in this field they always getting inspired me by own his words and behavior ,they always said that he was a biggest person in the world in future and also they purchase fruit and chocolate for me in anytime & anyway , firstly my father buy him then call me Vivek you want a chocolate i will say yes papa but how many tell me ,papa: you tell me how much i buy him i told 1 or 2 chocolate but my father purchase whole the boxes of chocolate and they get suprised me. MY FATHER WAS BORN IN " 20 SEPTEMBER" 1971 IN INDIA.

1) MY FATHER FAVORITE CLOTHES IS KURTA PAIJMA AND ALSO STYLES SHOE

2) FAVORITE SINGER IS KISHORE DA

3) FAVORITE STATE GUJARAT AND KOLKATA , HIS VILLAGE IN BIHAR

4) FAVORITE COLOR BLACK AND WHITE

THEY ALSO LOVE cricket like IPL and one day t-20 .they also like watching a News daily and heard the song daily ,they also interested in tik tok video but in current time tik tok is banned in india but also few videos are in you tube. In lockdown time my family and me very enjoy day daily. my father play daily ludo with his sister and son, daughter.they always loved tea and coffee anytime call me ". I make it tea for my father but some reason after the April to june they are suffering from fever and cough , weakness on 6 June 2020 my father death. they not told me say bye bye his life. After death of 6 June on 10 june my mom and dad anniversary.but my father is Best in the world they can do anything for me please take care of father and respect it of your parents.

1

Rishabh Pant

- Rishabh Pant

Rishabh Rajendra Pant (born 4 October 1997) is an Indian cricketer who plays as a middle order wicket-keeper batter for India, Delhi, and captains the Delhi Capitals in the Indian Premier League. He was the vice-captain of the India U-19 team for the 2016 Under-19 Cricket World Cup.

He made his Twenty20 International (T20I) debut for India in January 2017, his Test debut in August 2018, and his One Day International (ODI) debut in October 2018. In January 2019, Pant was named the ICC Men's Emerging Cricketer of the Year at the 2018 ICC Awards. In February 2021, Pant was named the Men's Player of the Month in the first edition of the ICC Player of the Month Awards.

In June 2022, Pant was named as the Indian captain for the T20I series against South Africa, after the designated captain KL Rahul was ruled of the series due to an injury.

- life

Rishabh Pant was born in Roorkee, Uttarakhand, India to Rajendra Pant and Saroj Pant. At the age of 12, Pant would travel with his mother to Delhi during the weekends to train with Tarak Sinha at the Sonnet Cricket Academy. He and his mother stayed at a Gurdwara in Moti Bagh as they did not have suitable accommodation in the city.

Sinha suggested Pant switch to Rajasthan to play U-13 and U-15 cricket but to no avail. Pant was instructed by his mentor to overhaul his entire batting technique in the hopes of becoming a better batsman. His turning point came when he was playing U-19 cricket for Delhi against Assam. Pant had top-scored with 35 in his first innings and then hit 150 in the second innings, which he claims was the most important knock in his career.

On 1 February 2016, during the 2016 Under-19 Cricket World Cup, Pant hit an 18-ball fifty against Nepal, the fastest at this level. Rishabh's father died in April 2017, due to a cardiac arrest.

· Domestic career

Pant made his first-class debut on 22 October 2015 in the 2015–16 Ranji Trophy and his List A debut the next month in the 2015–16 Vijay Hazare Trophy. In the 2016–17 Ranji Trophy, while playing a match against Maharashtra, Pant scored 308 runs in an innings, becoming the third-youngest Indian to score a triple century in first-class cricket.

On 8 November 2016, Pant scored the fastest century in the Ranji Trophy, from just 48 balls, in Delhi's match against Jharkhand.

In February 2017, Pant was named Delhi's captain for the 2016–17 Vijay Hazare Trophy. He took over from Gautam Gambhir, who led Delhi to the final of the previous season.

Delhi coach Bhaskar Pillai said it was a "consensus decision" to prepare Pant for the future.

On 14 January 2018, in the 2017–18 Zonal T20 League match between Himachal Pradesh and Delhi, Pant scored the second-fastest century in a Twenty20 match, making 100 from 32 balls.

- At Indian Premier League

Pant was purchased by the Delhi Daredevils ahead of the 2016 Indian Premier League on the same day he scored a century for India U-19 team in the 2016 Under-19 Cricket World Cup, guiding them into the semi-finals. Playing his third game of the season, Pant made 69 runs off 40 balls to help Delhi secure an eight-wicket victory over Gujarat Lions. In the 2017 season, he scored 97 runs from 43 balls against the same team.

During the 2018 Indian Premier League, Pant scored an unbeaten 128 from 63 balls against the Sunrisers Hyderabad, making it the then highest individual score by an Indian cricketer in IPL history. He also became the second youngest player to score a century in the IPL. In March 2021, Pant was named the captain of the Delhi Capitals for the 2021 Indian Premier League after the regular captain Shreyas Iyer was ruled out of the entire tournament due to an injury. He was retained as captain for the 2022 IPL season as well.

- International career Rishabh Pant wicket-keeping in India vs England series 2018

In January 2017, Pant was named in India's Twenty20 International (T20I) squad for their series against England.

He made his debut for India in the third T20I against England at the M. Chinnaswamy Stadium, Bangalore on 1 February 2017. Pant was the then youngest player to debut for India in a T20I match at the age of 19 years 120 days.

In February 2018, he was named in India's T20I squad for the 2018 Nidahas Trophy. In July 2018, Pant was named in India's Test squad for the series against England. He made his Test debut against England on 18 August 2018. He became the first batter for India to get off the mark in Test cricket with a six in the series. On 11 September 2018, Pant scored his maiden Test century, against England also becoming the second-youngest wicket-keeper and the first Indian wicket-keeper to score a Test century in England. The following month, he was named in India's One Day International (ODI) squad for their series against the West Indies. He made his ODI debut for India against the West Indies on 21 October 2018.

In December 2018, during the first Test against Australia, Pant took eleven catches, the most by a wicket-keeper for India in a Test match. In January 2019, during the fourth Test against Australia, Pant became the first wicket-keeper for India to score a century in a Test match in Australia.

In June 2019, Pant was called up to India's squad at the 2019 Cricket World Cup as a replacement for Shikhar Dhawan, who suffered a hairline fracture of his left thumb during India's game against Australia. Following the World Cup, the International Cricket Council (ICC) named Pant as the rising star of the squad.

In September 2019, during the second Test against the West Indies, Pant became the fastest wicket-keeper for India to affect fifty dismissals in Test cricket. In January 2021, during the fourth Test against Australia, Pant became the fastest wicket-keeper for India to reach 1,000 runs in

Test cricket.

- 2019-2020

The 2019–20 home season was billed as an important season for Pant with MS Dhoni announcing a hiatus from international cricket. India went into the season in search of a new wicket-keeping mainstay with Pant as one of the front-runners.However, ordinary performances from the left-hander and the emergence of KL Rahul as a wicket-keeping option meant that Pant slipped down the pecking order.

A dismal show in the 2020 IPL season didn't help either. Pant, who had scored a cumulative 1172 runs with a strike rate of 168 in the last two seasons, only managed to amass 343 runs with a strike rate of 113 His only fifty came in the finals in a losing cause.

Pant was consequently dropped from the limited-overs team touring Australia in 2020–21. He, however, kept his place in the Test team but did not make it to the playing eleven of the first Test in Adelaide.

During this period, Pant was heavily criticized by fans and the media. Disdainful comparisons with Indian cricket legend MS Dhoni were often brought up. There were instances of the crowd chanting "Dhoni! Dhoni!" when Pant made a mistake on the field.

India was bowled out for 36 in the second innings of the first Test of the Border Gavaskar Trophy 2020–21 and hence lost the test by 8 wickets despite getting a healthy first-innings lead. Following this, Rishabh Pant was picked ahead of Wriddhiman Saha for the second test in Melbourne.

While Pant scored 29 in the first innings of the Melbourne Test, it was at Sydney that he played a career-changing knock. With 97 overs to survive on the last day, he played a counter-attacking knock of 97 runs off just 118 balls, also putting up a 148-run partnership with Cheteshwar Pujara. The match ultimately ended in a draw.

India had many first-choice players unavailable due to injury, and were the underdogs going into the match played in The Gabba where Australia had not been defeated since 1988. Pant put in a match-winning performance on day five, as India chased down a target of 328 in the fourth innings, scoring an unbeaten 89.

In September 2021, Pant was named in India's squad for the 2021 ICC Men's T20 World Cup. At the annual ICC Awards in January 2022, Pant was named in ICC Men's Test Team of the Year for 2021. In March 2022, during the second match against Sri Lanka, Pant scored the fastest half-century by a batter for India in a Test match, breaking the record previously held by Kapil Dev. He brought up his half-century in just 28 deliveries.

In May 2022, Pant was named as the vice-captain of the Indian team for the South Africa tour of India 2022 series. However, one day before the first match of the series, Pant was named as the captain, after India's captain KL Rahul was ruled of the series out due to an injury. At the age of 24 years and 248 days, Pant became the second-youngest captain to lead India in a T20I match.

In July 2022, in the final match of India's tour of England, Pant recorded his maiden century in ODI cricket scoring 125 runs and remaining not out.

2
What Is Cricket ?

- What Is Cricket ?

Cricket is a bat-and-ball game played between two teams of eleven players on a field at the centre of which is a 22-yard (20-metre) pitch with a wicket at each end, each comprising two bails balanced on three stumps. The game proceeds when a player on the fielding team, called the bowler, "bowls" (propels) the ball from one end of the pitch towards the wicket at the other end. The batting side's players score runs by striking the bowled ball with a bat and running between the wickets, while the bowling side tries to prevent this by keeping the ball within the field and getting it to either wicket, and dismiss each batter (so they are "out"). Means of dismissal include being bowled, when the ball hits the stumps and dislodges the bails, and by the fielding side either catching a hit ball before it touches the ground, or hitting a wicket with the ball before a batter can cross the crease line in front of the wicket to complete a run. When ten batters have been dismissed, the innings ends and the teams swap roles. The game is adjudicated by two umpires, aided by a third umpire and match referee in international matches.

Forms of cricket range from Twenty20, with each team batting for a single innings of 20 overs and the game generally lasting three hours, to Test matches played over five days. Traditionally cricketers play in all-white kit, but in limited overs cricket they wear club or team colours. In addition to the basic kit, some players wear protective gear to prevent injury caused by the ball, which is a hard, solid spheroid made of compressed leather with a slightly raised sewn seam enclosing a cork core layered with tightly wound string.

The earliest reference to cricket is in South East England in the mid-16th century. It spread globally with the expansion of the British Empire, with the first international matches in the second half of the 19th century. The game's governing body is the International Cricket Council (ICC), which has over 100 members, twelve of which are full members who play Test matches. The game's rules, the Laws of Cricket, are maintained by Marylebone Cricket Club (MCC) in London. The sport is followed primarily in South Asia, Australasia, the United Kingdom, southern Africa and the West Indies.Women's cricket, which is organised and played separately, has also achieved international standard. The most successful side playing international cricket is Australia, which has won seven One Day International trophies, including five World Cups, more than any other country and has been the top-rated Test side more than any other country.

- History of cricket to 1725

A medieval "club ball" game involving an underhand bowl towards a batter. Ball catchers are shown positioning themselves to catch a ball. Detail from the Canticles of Holy Mary, 13th century.

Cricket is one of many games in the "club ball" sphere that basically involve hitting a ball with a hand-held implement; others include baseball (which shares many similarities with cricket, both belonging in the more specific bat-and-ball games category), golf, hockey, tennis, squash, badminton and table tennis. In cricket's case, a key difference is the existence of a solid target structure, the wicket (originally, it is thought, a "wicket gate" through which sheep were herded), that the batter must defend. The cricket historian Harry Altham identified three "groups" of "club ball" games: the "hockey group", in which the ball is driven to and fro between two targets (the goals); the "golf group", in which the ball is driven towards an undefended target (the hole); and the "cricket group", in which "the ball is aimed at a mark (the wicket) and driven away from it".

It is generally believed that cricket originated as a children's game in the south-eastern counties of England, sometime during the medieval period.Although there are claims for prior dates, the earliest definite reference to cricket being played comes from evidence given at a court case in Guildford in January 1597 (Old Style), equating to January 1598 in the modern calendar. The case concerned ownership of a certain plot of land and the court heard the testimony of a 59-year-old coroner, John Derrick, who gave witness that.

Being a scholler in the ffree schoole of Guldeford hee and diverse of his fellows did runne and play there at creckett and other plaies.

Given Derrick's age, it was about half a century earlier when he was at school and so it is certain that cricket was being played c. 1550 by boys in Surrey. The view that it was originally a children's game is reinforced by Randle Cotgrave's 1611 English-French dictionary in which he defined the noun "crosse" as "the crooked staff wherewith boys play at cricket" and the verb form "crosser" as "to play at cricket".

One possible source for the sport's name is the Old English word "cryce" (or "cricc") meaning a crutch or staff. In Samuel Johnson's Dictionary, he derived cricket from "cryce, Saxon, a stick". In Old French, the word "criquet" seems to have meant a kind of club or stick. Given the strong medieval trade connections between south-east England and the County of Flanders when the latter belonged to the Duchy of Burgundy, the name may have been derived from the Middle Dutch (in use in Flanders at the time) "krick"(-e), meaning a stick (crook). Another possible source is the Middle Dutch word "krickstoel", meaning a long low stool used for kneeling in church and which resembled the long low wicket with two stumps used in early cricket. According to Heiner Gillmeister, a European language expert of Bonn University, "cricket" derives from the Middle Dutch phrase for hockey, met de (krik ket)sen (i.e., "with the stick chase"). Gillmeister has suggested that not only the name but also the sport itself may be of Flemish origin.

- Growth of amateur and professional cricket in England

Evolution of the cricket bat. The original "hockey stick" (left) evolved into the straight bat from c. 1760 when pitched delivery bowling began.

Although the main object of the game has always been to score the most runs, the early form of cricket differed from the modern game in certain key technical aspects; the North American variant of cricket known as wicket retained many of these aspects. The ball was bowled underarm by the bowler and along the ground towards a batter armed with a bat that in shape resembled a hockey stick; the batter defended a low, two-stump wicket; and runs were called notches because the scorers recorded them by notching tally sticks.

In 1611, the year Cotgrave's dictionary was published, ecclesiastical court records at Sidlesham in Sussex state that two parishioners, Bartholomew Wyatt and Richard Latter, failed to attend church on Easter Sunday because they were playing cricket. They were fined 12d each and ordered to do penance.This is the earliest mention of adult participation in cricket and it was around the same time that the earliest known organised inter-parish or village match was played – at Chevening, Kent. In 1624, a player called Jasper Vinall died after he was accidentally struck on the head during a match between two parish teams in Sussex.

Cricket remained a low-key local pursuit for much of the 17th century. It is known, through numerous references found in the records of ecclesiastical court cases, to have been proscribed at times by the Puritans before and during the Commonwealth. The problem was nearly always the issue of Sunday play as the Puritans considered cricket to be "profane" if played on the Sabbath, especially if large crowds or gambling were involved.

According to the social historian Derek Birley, there was a "great upsurge of sport after the Restoration" in 1660. Gambling on sport became a problem significant enough for Parliament to pass the 1664 Gambling Act, limiting stakes to £100 which was, in any case, a colossal sum exceeding the annual income of 99% of the population. Along with prizefighting, horse racing and blood sports, cricket was perceived to be a gambling sport.Rich patrons made matches for high stakes, forming teams in which they engaged the first professional players.By the end of the century, cricket had developed into a major sport that was spreading throughout England and was already being taken abroad by English mariners and colonisers – the earliest reference to cricket overseas is dated 1676. A 1697 newspaper report survives of "a great cricket match" played in Sussex "for fifty guineas apiece" – this is the earliest known contest that is generally considered a First Class match.

- The patrons, and other players from the social class known as the "gentry", began to classify themselves as "amateurs" to establish a clear distinction from the professionals, who were invariably members of the working class, even to the point of having separate changing and dining facilities. The gentry, including such high-ranking nobles as the Dukes of Richmond, exerted their honour code of noblesse oblige to claim rights of leadership in any sporting contests they took part in, especially as it was necessary for them to play alongside their "social inferiors" if they were to win their bets. In time, a perception took hold that the typical amateur who played in first-class cricket, until 1962 when amateurism was abolished, was someone with a public school education who had then gone to one of Cambridge or Oxford University – society insisted that such people were "officers and gentlemen" whose destiny was to provide leadership. In a purely financial sense, the cricketing amateur would theoretically claim expenses for playing while his professional counterpart played under contract and was paid a wage or match fee; in practice, many amateurs claimed more than actual expenditure and the derisive term "shamateur" was coined to describe the practice.

- The Young Cricketer, 1768

The game underwent major development in the 18th century to become England's national sport.Its success was underwritten by the twin necessities of patronage and betting. Cricket was prominent in London as early as 1707 and, in the middle years of the century, large crowds flocked to matches on the Artillery Ground in Finsbury. The single wicket form of the sport attracted huge crowds and wagers to match, its popularity peaking in the 1748 season. Bowling underwent an evolution around 1760 when bowlers began to pitch the ball instead of rolling or skimming it towards the batter. This caused a revolution in bat design because, to deal with the bouncing ball, it was necessary to introduce the modern straight bat in place of the old "hockey stick" shape.

The Hambledon Club was founded in the 1760s and, for the next twenty years until the formation of Marylebone Cricket Club (MCC) and the opening of Lord's Old Ground in 1787, Hambledon was both the game's greatest club and its focal point. MCC quickly became the sport's premier club and the custodian of the Laws of Cricket. New Laws introduced in the latter part of the 18th century included the three stump wicket and leg before wicket (lbw).

The 19th century saw underarm bowling superseded by first roundarm and then overarm bowling. Both developments were controversial.Organisation of the game at county level led to the creation of the county clubs, starting with Sussex in 1839. In December 1889, the eight leading county clubs formed the official County Championship, which began in 1890.

The most famous player of the 19th century was W. G. Grace, who started his long and influential career in 1865. It was especially during the career of Grace that the distinction between amateurs and professionals became blurred by the existence of players like him who were nominally amateur but, in terms of their financial gain, de facto professional. Grace himself was said to have been paid more money for playing cricket than any professional.

The last two decades before the First World War have been called the "Golden Age of cricket". It is a nostalgic name prompted by the collective sense of loss resulting from the war, but the period did produce some great players and memorable matches, especially as organised competition at county and Test level developed.

• Cricket becomes an international sport

In 1844, the first-ever international match took place between the United States and Canada. In 1859, a team of English players went to North America on the first overseas tour. Meanwhile, the British Empire had been instrumental in spreading the game overseas and by the middle of the 19th century it had become well established in Australia, the Caribbean, India, Pakistan, New Zealand, North America and South Africa.

In 1862, an English team made the first tour of Australia. The first Australian team to travel overseas consisted of Aboriginal stockmen who toured England in 1868. The first One Day International match was played on 5 January 1971 between Australia and England at the Melbourne Cricket Ground.

In 1876–77, an England team took part in what was retrospectively recognised as the first-ever Test match at the Melbourne Cricket Ground against Australia. The rivalry between England and Australia gave birth to The Ashes in 1882, and this has remained Test cricket's most famous contest. Test cricket began to expand in 1888–89 when South Africa played England.

• World cricket in the 20th century

The inter-war years were dominated by Australia's Don Bradman, statistically the greatest Test batter of all time. Test cricket continued to expand during the 20th century with the addition of the West Indies (1928), New Zealand (1930) and India (1932) before the Second World War and then Pakistan (1952), Sri Lanka (1982), Zimbabwe (1992), Bangladesh (2000), Ireland and Afghanistan (both 2018) in the post-war period. South Africa was banned from international cricket from 1970 to 1992 as part of the apartheid boycott.

• The rise of limited overs cricket

Cricket entered a new era in 1963 when English counties introduced the limited overs variant. As it was sure to produce a result, limited overs cricket was lucrative and the number of matches increased. The first Limited Overs

International was played in 1971 and the governing International Cricket Council (ICC), seeing its potential, staged the first limited overs Cricket World Cup in 1975. In the 21st century, a new limited overs form, Twenty20, made an immediate impact. On 22 June 2017, Afghanistan and Ireland became the 11th and 12th ICC full members, enabling them to play Test cricket.

- A typical cricket field.

In cricket, the rules of the game are specified in a code called The Laws of Cricket (hereinafter called "the Laws") which has a global remit. There are 42 Laws (always written with a capital "L"). The earliest known version of the code was drafted in 1744 and, since 1788, it has been owned and maintained by its custodian, the Marylebone Cricket Club (MCC) in London.

- Playing area

Cricket is a bat-and-ball game played on a cricket field between two teams of eleven players each. The field is usually circular or oval in shape and the edge of the playing area is marked by a boundary, which may be a fence, part of the stands, a rope, a painted line or a combination of these; the boundary must if possible be marked along its entire length.

In the approximate centre of the field is a rectangular pitch (see image, below) on which a wooden target called a wicket is sited at each end; the wickets are placed 22 yards (20 m) apart. The pitch is a flat surface 10 feet (3.0 m) wide, with very short grass that tends to be worn away as the game progresses (cricket can also be played on artificial surfaces, notably matting). Each wicket is made of three wooden stumps topped by two bails.

- Cricket pitch and creases

As illustrated above, the pitch is marked at each end with four white painted lines: a bowling crease, a popping crease and two return creases. The three stumps are aligned centrally on the bowling crease, which is eight feet eight inches long. The popping crease is drawn four feet in front of the bowling crease and parallel to it; although it is drawn as a twelve-foot line (six feet either side of the wicket), it is, in fact, unlimited in length. The return creases are drawn at right angles to the popping crease so that they intersect the ends of the bowling crease; each return crease is drawn as an eight-foot line, so that it extends four feet behind the bowling crease, but is also, in fact, unlimited in length.

Before a match begins, the team captains (who are also players) toss a coin to decide which team will bat first and so take the first innings. Innings is the term used for each phase of play in the match.In each innings, one team bats, attempting to score runs, while the other team bowls and fields the ball, attempting to restrict the scoring and dismiss the batters. When the first innings ends, the teams change roles; there can be two to four innings depending upon the type of match. A match with four scheduled innings is played over three to five days; a match with two scheduled innings is usually completed in a single day. During an innings, all eleven members of the fielding team take the field, but usually only two members of the batting team are on the field at any given time. The exception to this is if a batter has any type of illness or injury restricting his or her ability to run, in this case the batter is allowed a runner who can run between the wickets when the batter hits a scoring run or runs,though this does not apply in international cricket. The order of batters is usually announced just before the match, but it can be varied.

The main objective of each team is to score more runs than their opponents but, in some forms of cricket, it is also necessary to dismiss all of the opposition batters in their final innings in order to win the match, which would otherwise be drawn. If the team batting last is all out having scored fewer runs than their opponents, they are said to have "lost by n runs" (where n is the difference between the aggregate number of runs scored by the teams). If the team that bats last scores enough runs to win, it is said to have "won by n wickets", where n is the number of wickets left to fall. For example, a team that passes its opponents' total having lost six wickets (i.e., six of their batters have been dismissed) have won the match "by four wickets".

In a two-innings-a-side match, one team's combined first and second innings total may be less than the other side's first innings total. The team with the greater score is then said to have "won by an innings and n runs", and does not need to bat again: n is the difference between the two teams' aggregate scores. If the team batting last is all out, and both sides have scored the same number of runs, then the match is a tie; this result is quite rare in matches of two innings a side with only 62 happening in first-class matches from the earliest known instance in 1741 until January 2017. In the traditional form of the game, if the time allotted for the match expires before either side can win, then the game is declared a draw.

If the match has only a single innings per side, then a maximum number of overs applies to each innings. Such a match is called a "limited overs" or "one-day" match, and the side scoring more runs wins regardless of the number of wickets lost, so that a draw cannot occur. In some cases, ties are broken by having each team bat for a one-over innings known as a Super Over; subsequent Super Overs may be played if the first Super Over ends in a tie. If this kind of match is temporarily interrupted by bad weather, then a complex mathematical formula, known as the Duckworth–Lewis–Stern method after its developers, is often used to recalculate a new target score. A one-day match can also be declared a "no-result" if fewer than a previously agreed number of overs have been bowled by either team, in circumstances that make normal resumption of play impossible; for example, wet weather.

In all forms of cricket, the umpires can abandon the match if bad light or rain makes it impossible to continue. There have been instances of entire matches, even Test matches scheduled to be played over five days, being lost to bad weather without a ball being bowled: for example, the third Test of the 1970/71 series in Australia.

- Innings

The innings (ending with 's' in both singular and plural form) is the term used for each phase of play during a match. Depending on the type of match being played, each team has either one or two innings. Sometimes all eleven members of the batting side take a turn to bat but, for various reasons, an innings can end before they have all done so. The innings terminates if the batting team is "all out", a term defined by the Laws: "at the fall of a wicket or the retirement of a batter, further balls remain to be bowled but no further batter is available to come in". In this situation, one of the batters has not been dismissed and is termed not out; this is because he has no partners left and there must always be two active batters while the innings is in progress.

- An innings may end early while there are still two not out batters

the batting team's captain may declare the innings closed even though some of his players have not had a turn to bat: this is a tactical decision by the captain, usually because he believes his team have scored sufficient runs and need time to dismiss the opposition in their innings

the set number of overs (i.e., in a limited overs match) have been bowled

the match has ended prematurely due to bad weather or running out of time

in the final innings of the match, the batting side has reached its target and won the game.

- Overs

The Laws state that, throughout an innings, "the ball shall be bowled from each end alternately in overs of 6 balls". The name "over" came about because the umpire calls "Over!" when six balls have been bowled. At this point, another bowler is deployed at the other end, and the fielding side changes ends while the batters do not. A bowler cannot bowl two successive overs, although a bowler can (and usually does) bowl alternate overs, from the same end, for several overs which are termed a "spell". The batters do not change ends at the end of the over, and so the one who was non-striker is now the striker and vice versa. The umpires also change positions so that the one who was at "square leg" now stands behind the wicket at the non-striker's end and vice versa.

- Clothing and equipment

English cricketer W. G. Grace "taking guard" in 1883. His pads and bat are very similar to those used today. The gloves have evolved somewhat. Many modern players use more defensive equipment than were available to Grace, most notably helmets and arm guards.

The wicket-keeper (a specialised fielder behind the batter) and the batters wear protective gear because of the hardness of the ball, which can be delivered at speeds of more than 145 kilometres per hour (90 mph) and presents a major health and safety concern. Protective clothing includes pads (designed to protect the knees and shins), batting gloves or wicket-keeper's gloves for the hands, a safety helmet for the head and a box for male players inside the trousers (to protect the crotch area). Some batters wear additional padding inside their shirts and trousers such as thigh pads, arm pads, rib protectors and shoulder pads. The only fielders allowed to wear protective gear are those in positions very close to the batter (i.e., if they are alongside or in front of him), but they cannot wear gloves or external leg guards.

Subject to certain variations, on-field clothing generally includes a collared shirt with short or long sleeves; long trousers; woolen pullover (if needed); cricket cap (for fielding) or a safety helmet; and spiked shoes or boots to increase traction. The kit is traditionally all white and this remains the case in Test and first-class cricket but, in limited overs cricket, team colours are worn instead.

- Bat and ball

Two types of cricket ball, both of the same size:
i) A used white ball. White balls are mainly used in limited overs cricket, especially in matches played at night, under floodlights (left).

ii) A used red ball. Red balls are used in Test cricket, first-class cricket and some other forms of cricket (right).

The essence of the sport is that a bowler delivers (i.e., bowls) the ball from his or her end of the pitch towards the batter who, armed with a bat, is "on strike" at the other end (see next sub-section: Basic gameplay).

The bat is made of wood, usually Salix alba (white willow), and has the shape of a blade topped by a cylindrical handle. The blade must not be more than 4.25 inches (10.8 cm) wide and the total length of the bat not more than 38 inches (97 cm). There is no standard for the weight, which is usually between 2 lb 7 oz and 3 lb (1.1 and 1.4 kg).

The ball is a hard leather-seamed spheroid, with a circumference of 9 inches (23 cm). The ball has a "seam": six rows of stitches attaching the leather shell of the ball to the string and cork interior. The seam on a new ball is prominent and helps the bowler propel it in a less predictable manner. During matches, the quality of the ball deteriorates to a point where it is no longer usable; during the course of this deterioration, its behaviour in flight will change and can influence the outcome of the match. Players will, therefore, attempt to modify the ball's behaviour by modifying its physical properties. Polishing the ball and wetting it with sweat or saliva is legal, even when the polishing is deliberately done on one side only to increase the ball's swing through the air, but the acts of rubbing other substances into the ball, scratching the surface or picking at the seam are illegal ball tampering.

• Player roles

Basic gameplay: bowler to batter

During normal play, thirteen players and two umpires are on the field. Two of the players are batters and the rest are all eleven members of the fielding team. The other nine players in the batting team are off the field in the pavilion. The image with overlay below shows what is happening when a ball is being bowled and which of the personnel are on or close to the pitch.

• Return crease

In the photo, the two batters (3 & 8; wearing yellow) have taken position at each end of the pitch (6). Three members of the fielding team (4, 10 & 11; wearing dark blue) are in shot. One of the two umpires (1; wearing white hat) is stationed behind the wicket (2) at the bowler's (4) end of the pitch. The bowler (4) is bowling the ball (5) from his end of the pitch to the batter at the other end who is called the "striker". The other batter (3) at the bowling end is called the "non-striker". The wicket-keeper (10), who is a specialist, is positioned behind the striker's wicket (9) and behind him stands one of the fielders in a position called "first slip" (11). While the bowler and the first slip are wearing conventional kit only, the two batters and the wicket-keeper are wearing protective gear including safety helmets, padded gloves and leg guards (pads).

While the umpire (1) in shot stands at the bowler's end of the pitch, his colleague stands in the outfield, usually in or near the fielding position called "square leg", so that he is in line with the popping crease (7) at the striker's end of the pitch. The bowling crease (not numbered) is the one on which the wicket is located between the return creases (12). The bowler (4) intends to hit the wicket (9) with the ball (5) or, at least, to prevent the striker (8) from scoring runs. The striker (8) intends, by using his bat, to defend his wicket and, if possible, to hit the ball away from the pitch in order to score runs.

Some players are skilled in both batting and bowling, or as either or these as well as wicket-keeping, so are termed all-rounders. Bowlers are classified according to their style, generally as fast bowlers, seam bowlers or spinners. Batters are classified according to whether they are right-handed or left-handed.

• Fielding

Of the eleven fielders, three are in shot in the image above. The other eight are elsewhere on the field, their positions determined on a tactical basis by the captain or the bowler. Fielders often change position between deliveries, again as directed by the captain or bowler.

If a fielder is injured or becomes ill during a match, a substitute is allowed to field instead of him, but the substitute cannot bowl or act as a captain, except in the case of concussion substitutes in international cricket. The substitute leaves the field when the injured player is fit to return. The Laws of Cricket were updated in 2017 to allow substitutes to act as wicket-keepers.

• Bowling and dismissal

Glenn McGrath of Australia holds the world record for most wickets in the Cricket World Cup.

Most bowlers are considered specialists in that they are selected for the team because of their skill as a bowler, although some are all-rounders and even specialist batters bowl occasionally. The specialists bowl several times during an innings but may not bowl two overs consecutively. If the captain wants a bowler to "change ends", another bowler must temporarily fill in so that the change is not immediate.

A bowler reaches his delivery stride by means of a "run-up" and an over is deemed to have begun when the bowler starts his run-up for the first delivery of that over, the ball then being "in play".

Fast bowlers, needing momentum, take a lengthy run up while bowlers with a slow delivery take no more than a couple of steps before bowling. The fastest bowlers can deliver the ball at a speed of over 145 kilometres per hour (90 mph) and they sometimes rely on sheer speed to try to defeat the batter, who is forced to react very quickly.

Other fast bowlers rely on a mixture of speed and guile by making the ball seam or swing (i.e. curve) in flight. This type of delivery can deceive a batter into miscuing his shot, for example, so that the ball just touches the edge of the bat and can then be "caught behind" by the wicket-keeper or a slip fielder. At the other end of the bowling scale is the spin bowler who bowls at a relatively slow pace and relies entirely on guile to deceive the batter. A spinner will often "buy his wicket" by "tossing one up" (in a slower, steeper parabolic path) to lure the batter into making a poor shot. The batter has to be very wary of such deliveries as they are often "flighted" or spun so that the ball will not behave quite as he expects and he could be "trapped" into getting himself out. In between the pacemen and the spinners are the medium paced seamers who rely on persistent accuracy to try to contain the rate of scoring and wear down the batter's concentration.

There are nine ways in which a batter can be dismissed: five relatively common and four extremely rare. The common forms of dismissal are bowled, caught, leg before wicket (lbw), run out and stumped. Rare methods are hit wicket,hit the ball twice, obstructing the field and timed out. The Laws state that the fielding team, usually the bowler in practice, must appeal for a dismissal before the umpire can give his decision. If the batter is out, the umpire raises a forefinger and says "Out!"; otherwise, he will shake his head and say "Not out".There is, effectively, a tenth method of dismissal, retired out, which is not an on-field dismissal as such but rather a retrospective one for which no fielder is credited.

· Batting, runs and extras

The directions in which a right-handed batter, facing down the page, intends to send the ball when playing various cricketing shots. The diagram for a left-handed batter is a mirror image of this one.

Batters take turns to bat via a batting order which is decided beforehand by the team captain and presented to the umpires, though the order remains flexible when the captain officially nominates the team. Substitute batters are generally not allowed, except in the case of concussion substitutes in international cricket.

In order to begin batting the batter first adopts a batting stance. Standardly, this involves adopting a slight crouch with the feet pointing across the front of the wicket, looking in the direction of the bowler, and holding the bat so it passes over the feet and so its tip can rest on the ground near to the toes of the back foot.

A skilled batter can use a wide array of "shots" or "strokes" in both defensive and attacking mode. The idea is to hit the ball to the best effect with the flat surface of the bat's blade. If the ball touches the side of the bat it is called an "edge". The batter does not have to play a shot and can allow the ball to go through to the wicketkeeper. Equally, he does not have to attempt a run when he hits the ball with his bat. Batters do not always seek to hit the ball as hard as possible, and a good player can score runs just by making a deft stroke with a turn of the wrists or by simply "blocking" the ball but directing it away from fielders so that he has time to take a run. A wide variety of shots are played, the batter's repertoire including strokes named according to the style of swing and the direction aimed: e.g., "cut", "drive", "hook", "pull".

The batter on strike (i.e. the "striker") must prevent the ball hitting the wicket, and try to score runs by hitting the ball with his bat so that he and his partner have time to run from one end of the pitch to the other before the fielding side can return the ball. To register a run, both runners must touch the ground behind the popping crease with either their bats or their bodies (the batters carry their bats as they run). Each completed run increments the score of both the team and the striker.

- Sachin Tendulkar is the only player to have scored one hundred international centuries

The decision to attempt a run is ideally made by the batter who has the better view of the ball's progress, and this is communicated by calling: usually "yes", "no" or "wait".

More than one run can be scored from a single hit: hits worth one to three runs are common, but the size of the field is such that it is usually difficult to run four or more. To compensate for this, hits that reach the boundary of the field are automatically awarded four runs if the ball touches the ground en route to the boundary or six runs if the ball clears the boundary without touching the ground within the boundary. In these cases the batters do not need to run. Hits for five are unusual and generally rely on the help of "overthrows" by a fielder returning the ball. If an odd number of runs is scored by the striker, the two batters have changed ends, and the one who was non-striker is now the striker. Only the striker can score individual runs, but all runs are added to the team's total.

Additional runs can be gained by the batting team as extras (called "sundries" in Australia) due to errors made by the fielding side. This is achieved in four ways: no-ball, a penalty of one extra conceded by the bowler if he breaks the rules; wide, a penalty of one extra conceded by the bowler if he bowls so that the ball is out of the batter's reach bye, an extra awarded if the batter misses the ball and it goes past the wicket-keeper and gives the batters time to run in the conventional way leg bye, as for a bye except that the ball has hit the batter's body, though not his bat. If the bowler has conceded a no-ball or a wide, his team incurs an additional penalty because that ball (i.e., delivery) has to be bowled again and hence the batting side has the opportunity to score more runs from this extra ball.

- Specialist roles

Captain (cricket) and Wicket-keeper

The captain is often the most experienced player in the team, certainly the most tactically astute, and can possess any of the main skillsets as a batter, a bowler or a wicket-keeper. Within the Laws, the captain has certain responsibilities in terms of nominating his players to the umpires before the match and ensuring that his players conduct themselves "within the spirit and traditions of the game as well as within the Laws".

The wicket-keeper (sometimes called simply the "keeper") is a specialist fielder subject to various rules within the Laws about his equipment and demeanour. He is the only member of the fielding side who can effect a stumping and is the only one permitted to wear gloves and external leg guards. Depending on their primary skills, the other ten players in the team tend to be classified as specialist batters or specialist bowlers. Generally, a team will include five or six specialist batters and four or five specialist bowlers, plus the wicket-keeper.

- Umpires and scorers

The game on the field is regulated by the two umpires, one of whom stands behind the wicket at the bowler's end, the other in a position called "square leg" which is about 15–20 metres away from the batter on strike and in line with the popping crease on which he is taking guard. The umpires have several responsibilities including adjudication on whether a ball has been correctly bowled (i.e., not a no-ball or a wide); when a run is scored; whether a batter is out (the fielding side must first appeal to the umpire, usually with the phrase "How's that?" or "Owzat?"); when intervals start and end; and the suitability of the pitch, field and weather for playing the game. The umpires are authorised to interrupt or even abandon a match due to circumstances likely to endanger the players, such as a damp pitch or deterioration of the light.

Off the field in televised matches, there is usually a third umpire who can make decisions on certain incidents with the aid of video evidence. The third umpire is mandatory under the playing conditions for Test and Limited Overs International matches played between two ICC full member countries. These matches also have a match referee whose job is to ensure that play is within the Laws and the spirit of the game.

The match details, including runs and dismissals, are recorded by two official scorers, one representing each team. The scorers are directed by the hand signals of an umpire . For example, the umpire raises a forefinger to signal that the batter is out (has been dismissed); he raises both arms above his head if the batter has hit the ball for six runs. The scorers are required by the Laws to record all runs scored, wickets taken and overs bowled; in practice, they also note significant amounts of additional data relating to the game.

A match's statistics are summarised on a scorecard. Prior to the popularisation of scorecards, most scoring was done by men sitting on vantage points cuttings notches on tally sticks and runs were originally called notches.According to Rowland Bowen, the earliest known scorecard templates were introduced in 1776 by T. Pratt of Sevenoaks and soon came into general use.It is believed that scorecards were printed and sold at Lord's for the first time in 1846.

· thank you for buy & read this book

have a great day of your
from : Mr Vivek Kumar Pandey

- This All Credit Goes To My Super Hero Daddy. "Always Love You dad'.

3
Rishabh Pant In Delhi Capitals

- Delhi Capitals

Delhi Capitals (formerly Delhi Daredevils) are a franchise cricket team based out of Delhi in the Indian Premier League (IPL). The franchise is jointly owned by the GMR Group and the JSW Group. The team's home ground is Arun Jaitley Stadium, located in New Delhi. The team is captained by Rishabh Pant and coached by Ricky Ponting. The Capitals appeared in their first IPL final in 2020.

The IPL is a cricket league organised by the Board of Control for Cricket in India (BCCI) and backed by the International Cricket Council (ICC). The inaugural tournament was held in April–June 2008, in which BCCI finalised a list of eight teams who participated in the tournament. The teams represented eight different cities in India, including Delhi. The teams were put up for auction in Mumbai on 20 February 2008, and the Delhi team was bought by the property development company GMR Group for US$84 million.

In March 2018, GMR sold a 50% stake in the Delhi Daredevils to JSW Sports for 550 crore (US$69 million).

In December 2018, the team changed its name from the Delhi Daredevils to the Delhi Capitals. Speaking to the rationale behind changing the team's name, co-owner and chairman Parth Jindal said, "Delhi is the power centre of the country, it is the capital, therefore the name Delhi Capitals." Co-owner Kiran Kumar Grandhi said, "The new name symbolizes Delhi's identity and just like the city, we are aiming to be the centre of all action going forward."

• Delhi Daredevils in 2008

During the inaugural edition of the IPL, the Delhi Daredevils won their initial two matches against the Rajasthan Royals and the Deccan Chargers. Then, after losing a match to the Kings XI Punjab, the team won their next two matches against the Royal Challengers Bangalore and the Chennai Super Kings.

However, the Delhi Daredevils lost in four straight matches, breaking the streak with a win against the Deccan Chargers. After another loss against the Kings XI Punjab, they recovered and won three matches to finish in the final four of the league.The Delhi Daredevils lost to eventual champions, the Rajasthan Royals, in the semi-final.

• Delhi Daredevils in 2009

The Daredevils dominated for much of the 2009 IPL season under the captaincy of former Indian opener and Delhi-native, Gautam Gambhir, finishing at the top of the table. The likes of former Indian opener and triple-

Centurion Sehwag and Gambhir had both developed since the prior season. They set up many large totals for the Daredevils, with South African power hitter and part-time keeper AB de Villiers hitting one of only two centuries in the 2009 IPL (the other was made by the young Indian batsman Manish Pandey) at a match in South Africa. The bowling team, which was composed mainly of New Zealander spin pro Daniel Vettori, India senior spinner Amit Mishra, Pradeep Sangwan, and former India fast bowler Ashish Nehra, was bolstered by the off-season signing of Australian Dirk Nannes, which created a strong bowling line-up. The batting of the Daredevils featured Sehwag, Gambhir, power hitter Dilshan, AB de Villiers, and Manoj Tiwary. The Daredevils consisted of new and then uncapped players like Australia Captain Aaron Finch and Australia all-rounder Glenn Maxwell, who went on to become successful in T20 circuits.

However, despite finishing at the top of the points table during the regular season, the Daredevils crumbled in the semi-final after Deccan Chargers' captain Adam Gilchrist hit the then fastest 50 in the IPL history (in just 17 balls). Nannes in particular, who was again picked over Aussie pacer Glenn McGrath, was punished by Gilchrist, and later by Aussie opening all-rounder Andrew Symonds. The semi-final loss meant Delhi did not contest the final of the 2009 IPL season, despite having the best record in the league stages. However, Delhi managed to qualify for the now-defunct 2009 Champions League Twenty20 as a result of their performance in the group stage.

• Delhi Daredevils in 2012

Due to the disbanding of the Kochi Tuskers Kerala, each team played the remaining eight teams twice, once at home and once away. Therefore, each team played an extended season of 16 matches.

In the 2012 IPL season, a new side of the Delhi Daredevils was seen after a poor 2011 season where they finished last. They came back strongly, having purchased players such as Afro-English batting great Kevin Pietersen, Sri Lanka batsman Mahela Jayawardene, and Kiwi batsman Ross Taylor. They stood first in the Pool Table with the Kolkata Knight Riders at second place, the Mumbai Indians coming third, and the defending champions the Chennai Super Kings securing the fourth spot, consequently also qualifying for the Champions League Twenty20 in 2012 held in South Africa.

Australian pace bowler Glenn McGrath expressed disappointment over not being picked to play any match during the whole season, and stopped playing for Delhi.

Former Sri Lankan skipper Mahela Jayawardane was appointed as the new captain of the Delhi Daredevils after Indian opener Virender Sehwag stepped down from captaincy during the 2012 season of the Champions League Twenty20.

· Delhi Daredevils in 2013

Delhi Daredevils lost their first six matches of IPL 2013 and won their first match in their seventh game against the Mumbai Indians. Virender Sehwag and Mahela Jayawardene's partnership led to a win against the Mumbai Indians, in which they scored 161 runs. Sehwag was the "Man of the Match" for his innings of 95* off 57 balls. After this match, they faced the Kings XI Punjab and lost again.

But in their ninth match of the season against the Pune Warriors India, they won, putting them in eighth place in the points table. They defeated defending champions the Kolkata Knight Riders in their tenth match by seven wickets but failed to advance to the seventh place due to their net run-rate. In their next match against the Sunrisers Hyderabad, the Delhi Daredevils were bowled out for just 80 runs, giving the Sunrisers a win. In their match against the Rajasthan Royals, they scored 154 runs, thanks to recruit Ben Rohrer's half-century. However, that effort was in vain as the Rajasthan Royals chased the total down with the loss of only one wicket. This loss for the Daredevils officially eliminated them from the 2013 season.

In their next match against the Royal Challengers Bangalore, Delhi managed to contain the Royal Challengers who were 106 in 16.0 overs, but Bangalore scored 77 in their last 4 overs and reached a total of 183, thanks to a 99 by RCB skipper Virat Kohli. The Daredevils lost the match by just four runs. The team next played the Chennai Super Kings who batted first and posted 168 runs. Delhi failed to gain momentum throughout the match and eventually lost by 33 runs. The following match was against the Kings XI Punjab who defeated them again, this time by seven runs, as they failed to chase down 172 runs. Their final game was against the Pune Warriors India. Delhi bowled first and the Pune Warriors posted a total of 171 runs. In the second innings, Delhi maintained the required run rate but began losing quick wickets after the tenth over. They could not chase the target and lost by 38 runs finishing last in the league table.

Despite seeing a forgettable season, a few big names were added to the support staff as the season progressed. The legendary West Indies batsman Sir Vivian Richards was named as their new brand ambassador, former

England spinner Jeremy Snape was added to the support staff, and renowned former Pakistan spinner Mushtaq Ahmed was named as their new spin bowling coach.

• Delhi Daredevils in 2014

Ahead of the IPL 2014 auction, on 10 January 2014, the Delhi Daredevils announced that they would not retain any players from their current squad for season seven. With no players retained, the team had the most "right-to-match" cards among all the franchises at the auction—three. They also had Rs 600 million (approx US$9.6 million) to spend at the auction.

The Delhi Daredevils experienced another poor season in 2014. They lost their first match, against the Royal Challengers Bangalore, however, they won their next match against the Kolkata Knight Riders. This was followed by a loss against the two-time champions the Chennai Super Kings and a close match which resulted in a loss against the Sunrisers Hyderabad. The Delhi Daredevils won their next match against the Mumbai Indians, having restricted them to 125. Later, when the tournament shifted from the makeshift venue in the United Arab Emirates (UAE) to India, Delhi lost their next nine matches. The Delhi Daredevils won only two out of their fourteen matches, both of which took place in the adopted venue in the UAE. Despite their poor performance, South Africa all-rounder JP Duminy, the team captain scored 410 runs from 14 matches at an average of 51.25 and was the tournament's eighth highest run-scorer. The Delhi Daredevils once again finished last.

• Delhi Daredevils in 2015

The team finished seventh in the 2015 edition of the IPL. They received fierce criticism from the Delhi fans due to their string of poor performances in the previous two years.

- Delhi Daredevils in 2016

The Delhi Daredevils released many of their players, including the previous year's most expensive purchase, all-rounder Yuvraj Singh, whom they had bought for 16 crores. The Daredevils also released former Sri Lankan skipper and all-rounder Angelo Mathews, who was bought for 7.5 crores. New additions to the team included uncapped all-rounder Pawan Negi, who was bought for 8.5 crores, thereby becoming the most expensive Indian player in the IPL auction of 2016.

Uncapped Indian batsman, Sanju Samson and Karun Nair, who previously played for the Rajasthan Royals, were also bought for hefty amounts. South African all-rounder Chris Morris was bought for 7 crores. English keeper Sam Billings and Australian Joel Paris also joined the Delhi squad. The team purchased three promising India U-19 players—local keeper Rishabh Pant, Rajasthan's pacer Khaleel Ahmed and Mahipal Lomror. After the Daredevils ended their association with South African batsman Gary Kirsten, they appointed Paddy Upton as their head coach. The Indian batsman and head coach of India U-19, Rahul Dravid was appointed the Daredevils' batting mentor. Former Indian pacer Zaheer Khan was appointed as the new captain of the Delhi Daredevils in the 2016 IPL season.

Relative to their performance in the previous three seasons, the Delhi Daredevils improved the way they played. South African all-rounder Chris Morris got the fastest 50 (17 balls) of the tournament and was also effective in the bowling department. South African wicket-keeper Quinton de Kock was among the leading run-scorers in the season. After losing their first match against two-time champions the Kolkata Knight Riders, the Daredevils went on to dominate the Kings XI Punjab, the Royal Challengers Bangalore, defending champions the Mumbai Indians, the Kolkata Knight Riders in the second leg, and newcomers the Gujarat Lions. They won 5 of their first 7 matches, gaining 10 points. They lost their second match against newcomers the Gujarat Lions by just one run. The Daredevils were the favourites to qualify for the playoffs; however, they finished in sixth with fourteen points in fourteen games.

· Delhi Daredevils in 2017

Delhi lost South Africans de Kock and Duminy before the tournament, placing dependence on a young batting line-up and a bowling line-up of former Indian pacer Zaheer Khan, Indian pacer Mohammed Shami, South African all-rounder Chris Morris, Aussie bowling all-rounder Pat Cummins, South African young pacer Kagiso Rabada, Indian spinner Amit Mishra, young spinner Shahbaz Nadeem, Jayant Yadav and Ben Hilfenhaus. They lost to runners-up RCB in the first game and won by big margins against RPS and KXIP. After this, they lost five consecutive games. However, they bounced back by chasing 189 and 214 against defending champions SRH and GL respectively. Keralite wicket-keeper Sanju Samson got the first century of the season. Young wicket-keeper and local boy Rishabh Pant made 97 against GL. But the Delhi Daredevils lost to then two-time champions MI by a margin of 146 runs, which was the highest win by runs in the IPL history. During the middle of the tournament, captain and former Indian pacer Zaheer Khan was down with an injury to his hamstring which caused him to miss three matches, and young Indian batsman Karun Nair was appointed as stand-in captain.

The Delhi Daredevils ended up in the sixth position again with six wins (+12 points) and eight losses for the season.

• Delhi Daredevils in 2018

Going into the big auctions, each franchise were allowed to retain up to three players. Additionally, they could also use Right to Match cards to get back two players during the auctions. Delhi Daredevils retained Shreyas Iyer, Chris Morris and Rishabh Pant.Coach Rahul Dravid had to quit his job as the coach in order to protect his position as coach of India A and India U-19, following a conflict of interest debate. Ricky Ponting was appointed as the new coach.

• Delhi Capitals in 2019

The Delhi Capitals retained 14 players and traded their former player and India opener Shikhar Dhawan from Sunrisers Hyderabad. This was done by trading off the young all-rounder Vijay Shankar, and Abhishek Sharma and spinner Shahbaz Nadeem for the 12th season of the IPL. Retained players for the twelfth IPL season were: captain and Indian batsman Shreyas Iyer, Indian wicket-keeper and left-handed batsman Rishabh Pant, young Indian batsman Prithvi Shaw, Indian spinner Amit Mishra, young pacer Avesh Khan, uncapped bowler and injured Harshal Patel, uncapped bowling all-rounder Rahul Tewatia, Jayant Yadav, Manjot Kalra, New Zealand opener Colin Munro, New

Zealand pacer Trent Boult, South African all-rounder Chris Morris, young South African pacer Kagiso Rabada and young Nepalese spinner Sandeep Lamichhane.

On the IPL auction day, 18 December 2018, DC filled up their 10 available player slots (seven Indian slots and three overseas slots) with: South African batsman Colin Ingram, Indian all-rounder Axar Patel, Indian all-rounder Hanuma Vihari, Sherfane Rutherford, Indian pacer Ishant Sharma, West Indian pacer Keemo Paul, and uncapped Indian cricketers Jalaj Saxena, Ankush Bains, Nathu Singh and Bandaru Ayyappa.

Delhi Capitals also brought the former Indian captain Sourav Ganguly as their official advisor and later traded Jayant Yadav to the Mumbai Indians after the IPL 2019 auction.

The Capitals began their campaign with a 37-run victory over 3-time champions Mumbai. The Capitals entered the playoffs after seven years, and they won their first playoffs match against the Sunrisers Hyderabad by two wickets. They lost the second match against the Chennai Super Kings by six wickets and ended up as second runners up in the playoffs, their best-ever finish.

• Delhi Capitals in 2020

Delhi Capitals released Hanuma Vihari, Jalaj Saxena, Manjot Kalra, Ankush Bains, Nathu Singh, Bandaru Ayappa, Chris Morris, Colin Ingram, and Colin Munro from their 2019 roster.They have added Jason Roy, Chris Woakes , Alex Carey, Shimron Hetmyer, Mohit Sharma, Tushar Deshpande, Marcus Stoinis, and Lalit Yadav for their 2020 roster during the IPL Auction.Chris Woakes, however pulled out of the tournament and was replaced by South African fast bowler Anrich Nortje. Jason Roy, became the second player (and second English Player) from Capitals to pull out of the tournament due to injury concerns and personal reasons, he was replaced by Australian bowling all-rounder Daniel Sams.

The team started well in the tournament, winning 7 out of the first 9 games. However, a string of four losses in a row put them in a position where losing their last match could result in failure to make it to the playoffs. They however, were able to defeat Royal Challengers Bangalore in the last match and thus, finished as the second ranked team in league stage. Also, a win over Sunrisers Hyderabad in Qualifier 2 helped them reach the finals for the first time in the history of the IPL.In the finals, they were defeated by Mumbai Indians—the only team that Delhi could not defeat in the tournament despite playing them 4 times. Also, this was the most successful season for Delhi Capitals in the IPL history. In this season, all games were played in the UAE.

· Delhi Capitals in 2021

The 2021 IPL season was held in India. All teams were scheduled to play at neutral venues (no team played at their home ground). On 30 March 2021, Delhi Capitals officially promoted Rishabh Pant to captain of the squad after Shreyas Iyer dislocated his shoulder while fielding a ball in the ODI series against England and consequently, was ruled out of the 2021 IPL season. Delhi Capitals had 3 matches at the Wankhede Stadium, followed by 2 in Chennai, 4 in Ahmedabad and 5 in Kolkata. Delhi Capitals had won 6 games out of 8 matches and were placed at the top of the points table before the season was indefinitely suspended following a breach of the COVID-19 bio secure bubble.

· Home ground

The Delhi Capitals play their home matches in the Arun Jaitley Stadium located in New Delhi.They also have the modern Shaheed Veer Narayan Singh International Stadium, Raipur as their second home ground.

· Team anthems

Bollywood playback singer Kailash Kher was the artist for the team's anthem "Khelo Front Foot Pe" ("Play on the front foot") or "play aggressively".

The Delhi Daredevils launched their new anthem "Munday Dilli Ke" ("The Lads from Delhi"), sung by Jaspreet Jasz and composed by Arijit Datta and Micu Patel on 5 March 2012 on YouTube.

Their anthem for the 2016 season of IPL, titled "Dhuandaar Dilli" was released on YouTube, sung by Sukhwinder Singh.

In 2018, they released yet another theme song, titled "Dil Dilli hai, ab Dhadkega".

The theme song for the 2019 season for the rechristened franchise, the Delhi Capitals was "Roar Machaa" sung by Amit Trivedi.

· List of Delhi Daredevils cricketers

Former India Opener and Delhi local, Virender Sehwag was accorded the icon player status in the Delhi Daredevils team and was also the captain of the side during the first two seasons. However, he resigned and passed on the leadership to Gautam Gambhir for the 2010 season. But after Gambhir left the team for the Kolkata Knight Riders in the fourth edition, Sehwag was once again given the duty to captain the team. Since the start of the IPL in 2008, many international players such as Australian Glenn McGrath, South African batsman and part-time keeper AB de Villiers, Sri Lanka player Tillakaratne Dilshan, Australia opener and former vice-captain David Warner, Andrew McDonald, New Zealand spinner Daniel Vettori, Farveez Maharoof, Dirk Nannes and Aussie opener Aaron Finch have donned the cap for the Daredevils. The team included Indian players like Tamil Nadu Middle-order batsman and keeper Dinesh Karthik and Yo Mahesh.

In 2009, Mohammad Asif and Shoaib Malik left due to the ban on Pakistani players and Asif's positive drug test. Aussie opener David Warner, Andrew McDonald, English Opener Paul Collingwood and Owais Shah were the new signings. Fast bowler Ashish Nehra came in from Mumbai Indians as a trade-off for Indian Opener Shikhar Dhawan. For IPL 2010, Australian all-rounder Moises Henriques came in from the Kolkata Knight Riders in exchange for Manoj Tiwary and Owais Shah. Wayne Parnell was purchased at the auction for US$610,000.

In 2012, they bought Sri Lankan Mahela Jayawardene, Jamaican all-rounder Andre Russell, Doug Bracewell, Morne Morkel and English batsman Kevin Pietersen. The Daredevils also signed uncapped Indian all-rounder Pawan Negi, batsmen Manpreet Juneja and Kuldeep Rawal ahead of the 2012 season. The Daredevils appointed Mahela Jayawardene as vice-captain for 2012. On 29 February 2012, the Daredevils signed Kiwi Batsman Ross Taylor from the inaugural Champions Rajasthan Royals in a trade for an undisclosed amount. David Warner is most valuable player and highest runner in 2022

www.ingramcontent.com/pod-product-compliance
Lightning Source LLC
Chambersburg PA
CBHW021143130726
47988CB00003B/1445